TALKING TO MY GRAN
ABOUT DYING

MY SCHOOL PROJECT

Third Age Press

ISBN 978-1-898576-17-4
First edition

Third Age Press Ltd, 2010
Third Age Press, 6 Parkside Gardens
London SW19 5EY
www.thirdagepress.co.uk
Managing Editor Dianne Norton

Illustrations by Philip Jordan

Layout by Dianne Norton
Printed in Great Britain by IntypeLibra

TALKING TO MY GRAN
ABOUT DYING

MY SCHOOL PROJECT

Gina Levete

illustrated by
Philip Jordan

ABOUT THE AUTHOR

Gina Levete has a background in dance. After marriage she researched into the artistic needs of disabled and disadvantaged people in the UK.

She is the founder of **Shape UK**– an organisation to provide artistic opportunities for disabled and disadvantaged people.

This work lead to the publication of ***No Handicap To Dance*** published by Souvenir Press in 1982.

She then founded **Interlink** – an international free advisory service to help other countries make the arts more accessible to disadvantaged and disabled people within their communities and helped to set up a number of international projects including Interlink Calcutta based on the structure of Shape UK.

The Creative Tree was published by Michael Russell Publishing Ltd in 1987.

Gina's research into the problem of loneliness resulted in ***Letting Go of Loneliness*** published by Element Books Ltd in 1993.

Her contribution to ***Meditation in Schools – calmer classrooms,*** published by Continuum in 2001, was the result of her research into the potential of introducing the practice of meditation within schools.

TO ANYONE WHO READS MY DIARY

Hi, my name is Will.

This diary is for anyone who sometimes thinks about dying and sometimes wonders about what happens when people die.

I chose the subject of dying for my school project. That might seem a bit strange. But seeing as everyone and everything dies at some time, it's not really. The other reason I chose it was because it got me out of having to go to the library after school to look things up. All I did was talk about dying to my Granny, who I call Tam. Because she's seventy I guessed she would think about dying like everyday!

I'm glad I talked to Tam. She was glad too because there aren't many opportunities to talk about dying and find out what other people think.

I asked a lot of questions. Sometimes she didn't know the answer and thought it would be a good idea to ask anyone reading this diary the same questions.

So at the end of each talk there's a `What do you think` question for you and your Mum and Dad or grandparents or teacher to think about, and it might help if you write down what you think.

Will

The questions Tam and I talked about were:

YOU'LL HAVE PLENTY OF TIME TO DECIDE
ON YOUR PROJECT WHILE YOU ARE HERE

TALKING TO MY GRAN
ABOUT DYING

My name is Will. I'm ten years old. I go to Greenway Primary School. Greenway Primary is in Manchester. I'm a Man United supporter. Football is like half my life. Football is why I ended up in hospital with a broken leg.

Just before I broke my leg, Miss Evans, our class teacher, told us that moving up to Year Five meant working on our own school project. She said each of us could choose any subject except football.

I thought the only good thing about breaking a leg might mean getting out of having to do the project.

No chance. Second visitor after Mum was Miss Evans. She said 'Well Will, while you're here you'll have plenty of time to decide on your project'.

The boy in the next bed told me that if your bed was near the door (and mine was) it meant you might die because you were seriously ill. I found that scary. Really scary. I asked the nurse if what he said was true. She said that was rubbish.
She said patients were put where there happened to be a spare bed.

Anyway what the-boy-in-the-next-bed said got me thinking about what happens to people when they die. Then I thought 'Dying' could be my project!

Problem - where can I find out about dying? Mum's too busy working. Anyway don't expect she thinks about it much. She's only 38. But I guess my Gran Tam thinks about it everyday. She's 70. Instead of having to go to the library, all I've got to do is talk to Tam. Easy!

Back at school. Still on crutches. Really boring – no football! Miss Evans said I could make up for it by getting ahead with my project. She looked really surprised when I told her what it was going to be about. 'What made you choose that subject for your project?'

I couldn't tell her that I'd chosen it 'cos it's easier to talk to my Gran than go to the library after school. So I just said, 'Well there are things about dying that I want to know.' That was true. There are things about dying I want to know.

Then Miss Evans asked me what kind of things I wanted to know.

'Things like, where does a person go, and why do people have to die if they aren't old. Just things like that.'

'I'm not sure the library will have books on those kind of questions', she said. I could have told her that.

'That's why I'm going to talk to my Gran', I said. 'She's an old person who must be wondering what will happen to her after she's died'.

Miss Evans suggested I could present the project to the rest of Year 5 as a discussion topic. She even suggested I might read it out at assembly. Hope it never comes to that.

MY PROJECT

Beginning to think perhaps Miss Evans is worried about dying. She keeps looking over my shoulder as I write.

'When you write, be creative', she says.

I'm not sure dying is creative, 'cos . . . well it's like the end, isn't it?

Miss Evans pinches her lips up like she doesn't know what to say

Still can't play football. Sooo boring.

I was going to call my Gran Tam but Mum had to go to a funeral and I had to go too. Her best friend's partner had died. He was called Max. We took the train to Birmingham.

After the funeral Mum was a bit tearful in the train. I didn't know what to say. So to take her mind off things I asked her what happens when people die.

Mum looked like she was going to cry again, but she didn't. She said, 'When a person or an animal dies their heart stops beating and the body stops breathing. If that happens the brain no longer works. It is no longer conscious to be aware of what is going on around it.'

I asked her why people die. She said 'Most people die when they are very old because their body wears out like an old machine. Sometimes people of all ages die because of a serious illness that can't be cured, or because of events like wars, natural disasters or accidents.'

'Does dying hurt?' I ask.

'If a dying person is very ill or wounded, there is pain. But there are many drugs nowadays to stop pain. When we die there is no more pain. The body has just quietly shut down.'

I asked Mum if she has seen anyone dead. She said that she has seen one person. That was my Grandad. He was old and his heart stopped working.

Mum said 'When I saw your Grandad just after he died, he had a really peaceful look on his face. It was as if all his troubles and worries had flown away.'

I wanted to know for my project what happens to a person who has died. So I said 'Where do you think Max is now? I mean his body is in a coffin but . . . ?'

OOPS! Wrong question. Mum looked like she might cry again. The train was coming into Manchester Central so she didn't have to answer.

When we got home, I rang Gran Tam. Told her I need to talk to her about dying for the project.   Tam looks like someone seventy years old, but she says inside she feels more like seven years old.   Her knees are bad so she is not much good at kicking a football, but she is awesome in goal.

When we went to the Isle of Wight, she and I stood on the beach in the rain trying to pebble a coke can into the sea. Tam's all right.

On the phone, I asked if she thinks a lot about dying, because she is old; does she think about it everyday?

'Not everyday but I do from time to time', she said.

I told her I would be scared to die. 'Are you scared that you'll die at any time?'

Silence.

'Hope I haven't upset you Tam.'

'No. I was just thinking your project is a good idea because dying is a part of what it means to be alive. Dying happens to everyone. We are born. We live our lives and die. So our talks could really help me to understand this.'

MY FIRST TALK WITH TAM

Why do people have to die?

Tam and I are walking to the cycle shop to get a water container for my bike. She's buying it for me as part of my birthday present.

The sun is shining and the sky is blue (this creative bit should please Miss Evans). Can't hear the birds. I'd like to live in the country where you can hear the birds. Mum says she is a townie through and through, so no hope there.

I say to Tam 'I bet all these people walking down street don't want to die.'

Tam says no one wants to die, but the way nature works means everything in the universe is changing all the time – being born and dying. She says that in a hundred years nearly everyone we have passed in the street will have died!

Then she tells me – and this is really interesting – that our bodies are changing all the time. Even now as we are walking down the street.

'The tiny bits that make up the body are always dying and being replaced by new ones.' I tell Tam I know what the tiny bits are called – cells.

'When you think about it, Will, if things stayed the same there would be no room for anything new to be born or grow. There would be no new ideas, discoveries, or inventions. Everything in this universe is changing all the time. That includes the way we feel. When we are angry, that feeling passes. When we are excited, that feeling passes. Thoughts and feelings, like everything else, come and go.'

'Mum says scientists are discovering how old people will be able to live even longer, like into their hundreds. Would you like to live like to a hundred and fifty?'

Tam is silent - thinking about the question. Then she says 'Even if I could live to a hundred and fifty, eventually bodies wear out. Like flowers that fade and die. So I hope I live long enough to see you grow up, but after that I think I will be ready to be on my way.'

Arrive at cycle shop. Water container in window. Tell Tam to wait outside.

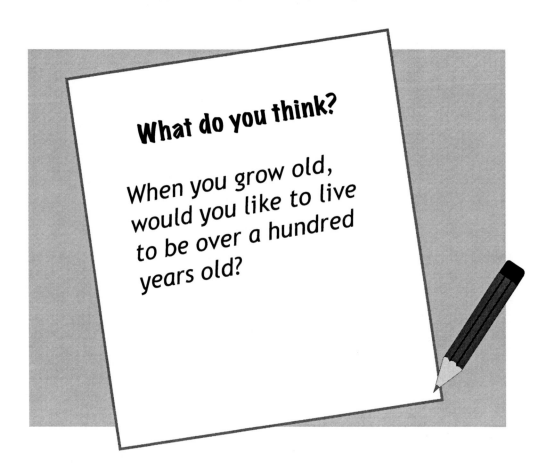

What do you think?

When you grow old, would you like to live to be over a hundred years old?

This is me not feeling well....

SECOND TALK WITH TAM
ABOUT DYING

Where do people go
when they die?

I'm not at school. I'm not well. Tam is round because Mum is at work. Playing Monopoly doesn't take my mind off feeling not well.

'Think I'll lie down for a bit', I say.

Later on Tam asks if I would like to do a bit more on the project. Seems like a good idea since today is turning out to be really boring.

'OK, where do people go after they die? I mean, what do you think happens to them? Mum says they leave their bodies behind or something like that.'

Tam tells me it's a difficult question to answer. 'People all over the world have different answers to this question. Sometimes, what they believe depends on their religious beliefs, if they are religious. Different religions have different beliefs about what happens.'

Some people believe that when the physical body dies there is something that is called a spirit or a soul, which leaves the body at the time of death.'

I remember what Mary in my class said. She told me her spirit will go to heaven if she is a good person.

Tam's still talking. 'Some people believe that when the body dies, the thing that makes us conscious, aware and thinking continues in another form. Perhaps another human form. They believe that being alive on this planet is like going to school to learn the lessons of life, and when those lessons have been learnt there will be no need to be born again.

'Some people think nothing happens after a person has died - that's it.'

Then there are people who think that when the body dies all that is left of us are the tiny parts of energy, called atoms that make up the body. These atoms whirl about the universe as part of other things.'

I start to think about atoms whirling about in space like when I first switch on our old TV and the screen looks like snowflakes.

My dad told me that the things that look like snowflakes are vibrations of energy that could have happened billions of years ago and have taken all this time to get to our planet. Melchi my best friend says he can't see snowflakes on his new flat screen TV. Mum says she's saving up for a flat screen. I can't wait.

Tam says she has only mentioned a few of the beliefs people have about what happens to them after they die.

Then she says 'There is one thing that seems the same whatever a person believes. Our physical body is like a house. A house to be alive in.'

I tell Tam that she hasn't said what she thinks will happen to her when she dies.

She says 'To be truthful Will, I don't know. I just don't know. What I do know is that talking to you has made me realise it also can be a real adventure not to know'

Feel better. Texting Melchi to ask if he can come round after school.

What do you think?

Have you ever thought about what happens to people or pets after they die?

THIRD TALK WITH TAM
ABOUT DYING

Why do people have to die
when they are not old?

I wasn't nice to Tam today. The reason I wasn't nice to her today is today is Friday. On Fridays Mum leaves work early. She meets me from school and we go and have hot chocolate.

But today Tam is at the gate holding up her broken umbrella. Wish she would buy a new one.

'I thought Mum was coming', I say in a way that means why did you have to come.

'She had to stay on at work because of some emergency.'

Tam sees the bruise on my face. 'How did you get that?'

'Melchi and me had a friendly fight, then David came along and started a real fight. Then the teacher on duty sent us all to the head teacher.'

Still in a bad mood, I start walking down the street fast. I know Tam won't be able to keep up because of her knees. Then I think it's not her fault she's here.

'Miss Evans says we have to hand in our projects soon like soon. I told Melchi I was talking to you about dying. He said it's weird and sad to talk about dying.'

Tam asks me if it makes me sad.

I say 'Not really, but then I'm not going to die.'

Then I remember something I really want to know.

'Why can't it be only older people who have to die? Begonia, she's in my class, well her brother died when he was only 10.'

Tam shakes her head like she may not be able to help with this part of my project.

Then she says, 'Children and people of all ages die because of illness, accidents, wars famines and other disasters.   I don't know why things happen like this and I wonder if anyone does. So these are some of my 'maybe' thoughts:

● maybe dying before you are old seems so very sad because most of us cannot imagine anything else except to be alive as we are.

• maybe living on this planet is like going to school to learn, and those who die young are very special people who do not need to learn all the lessons of life that we spoke about before.

• maybe dying is just another step on a journey to something so wonderful we cannot imagine.

• maybe we need to understand everything in the universe is a form of energy. Energy gives life to everything, like the body of a footballer, an insect, a tree, and a little weed pushing through a crack in a pavement. So even when someone or something dies, that energy flows on to something else.

What Tam has just said gets me thinking about what energy is and how you can't see it. I might ask Mr Till. He teaches science to Year 6.

Mum is coming up the street. I run to meet her. My homework falls out of my school bag onto the wet pavement. This project diary is now soggy grey. Miss Evans will go crazy.

What do you think?

Do you have any 'maybe' thoughts about death?

FOURTH TALK WITH TAM ABOUT DYING

Is it OK to forget people and pets who have died?

I ring Tam to ask if she would like to see the scooter that my Dad has given me. Dad and Mum are divorced but they still like each other. Mum likes his new partner. I like her too. Mum has a new friend. Not sure if I like him.

On the phone I say 'Tam, I'll bring my scooter. Then we can go to the cemetery and I can finish my project.'

When we meet I demonstrate my skills on the scooter. Tam asks if she can have a go.

'Sure', I say.

Tam starts to scoot and lifts one leg in the air like she thinks she is a ballet dancer. Then she wobbles and scoots right into a black plastic bag full of rubbish. Am I glad none of my friends can see this!

To get to the cemetery, we go by the river walk way and then through a little gate. I have to push the scooter because of weeds on the path. There are all these graves, some of them so old they're half buried in the ground. Hardly any have flowers. Tam and I read the messages on the stones.

This one says, 'Mary Anderson born 1920 died 1982. Buried next to her beloved husband Harry. Rest in peace. We love you Mum and Dad. Mark and Jennifer'.

I say to Tam that I think Mark and Jennifer must have forgotten their Mum and Dad because there are no flowers, just weeds around the grave.

It's a hot day so we sit down by Mary Anderson's grave. I wonder whether when people die they feel homesick, missing their family. I ask Tam if she thinks she will miss me.

'I think when my body dies those kinds of feelings won't be there anymore.'

There is something else I'm going to tell Tam. That is that when she dies sometimes I may forget her. 'Do you mind?'

Tam shakes her head. She says that as time goes by, it's natural to sometimes forget the people or pets we love. 'It's nature's way of helping heal our grief so that we can carry on enjoying our own adventure of being alive.'

I tell Tam that the other day in the playground Begonia told me that sometimes she feels bad about being alive because her brother is dead.

Tam says that it's normal to feel like that. And it's OK.

She says 'We never truly forget people we really love. It's like having two pockets. In one pocket we keep happy memories about the person who has died and some sad feelings about missing them. In the other pocket are all the things to do with the fun of being alive. The good thing is that we can think about either pocket whenever we like. Even both pockets at the same time!'

I tell Tam that we need only have one more talk before I hand in the project to Miss Evans.

We start walking back. Tam pushes the gate open. She says 'You know, coming here with you has given me a friendly feeling.'

'Why?' I ask.

She says 'Well, coming here and seeing all the graves reminds me that at some time or other dying happens to every thing and everyone. It happens to prime ministers, film stars, pop stars, footballers, animals, plants and everything we see around us.

Back on the river walk, I see Melchi coming towards us on his cycle. He invites me over to his place. Tam says it's OK for me to go. Tam sits by the river. She likes sunshine.

What do you think?

Is it OK to forget people or pets who have died?

FIFTH TALK WITH TAM ABOUT DYING

The last talk

Tam chooses to meet in the park for the last talk. She says the park because there are conkers on the trees, and the leaves are turning gold brown. Tam likes autumn.

'This is a good place to meet for the last talk because everything in the park is saying goodbye to summer. Everything is getting ready to change so that something new can begin. The leaves are falling; the gardeners are pulling up the summer flowers.'

'Like what you said about dying to make room for new things to be born?' I ask.

'Yes' she says. 'When summer comes again it will be a new summer.'

I like kicking through the leaves that have dropped on the ground. I like the noise the leaves make when I walk through them.

I look down because my foot has kicked something soft. 'Look Tam, it's a dead sparrow.'

Tam's looking at the sparrow. 'Do you think it looks like a sparrow now?' she asks.

'No, it just seems like something dead, not sparrow. I guess its life energy has flown somewhere, maybe to another body or into space.'

Tam has an idea: 'If we leave the sparrow's body here it will turn to dust like these fallen leaves as they soak into the ground. The sparrow's body will be nourishing the roots of this tree. So you could say that by next springtime this sparrow body would be part of the tree and its leaves.'

I like what Tam has just said.

Then she says she read in a little book that everything in the universe is in everything else. The person who wrote the book said we should think about a piece of paper. Paper is made from trees. Trees need space, air, sunlight, rain, and soil to grow. A piece of paper is made from all these things.

All things that are in a piece of paper...

sun

rain

tree

earth

← paper

I find that quite interesting. I never thought about paper in that way. If that's right, then if this tree is cut down for paper, that paper will have sparrow body in it too!

I ask Tam if this project has helped her not to be afraid to die. She hugs me like she is really pleased.

She says that talking about dying has helped her to really understand dying is part of the adventure of being alive. 'We know that everything that is born dies. We may not understand why this has to be but it is a fact. Nothing lasts or stays the same. Everything changes. It's all part of our adventure, Will.'

Tam has a big smile on her face when she says this. I do too but for another reason. Tam and me are going to Starbucks to have hot chocolate and chocolate fudge cake.

I can't wait for Monday. Not because I can hand in my school project to Miss Evans, but because the doctor says I can play football again!

What do you think?

Do you think talking about death and dying is a good idea or not? Please say why.

NOTES FOR ADULTS

This book is for children (mainly aged 8 – 12). The purpose of the book is to open up the subject of death in a way that encourages discussion and debate in the classroom or home. Within the curriculum, it fits in the fields of philosophy for children, critical thinking and Personal Health and Social Education (PHSE).

Death is still a relatively taboo subject for open debate, despite the fact that at some point it will happen to us all. Thinking and talking about it can be helpful both for children who have experienced the loss of a loved one, and children who are naturally curious or have unexpressed anxiety to do with dying.

Talking to My Gran about Dying is the diary of Will who chooses the subject of death for his school project partly because there are things he wants to know, and partly because it will get him out of having to do research in the library after school. Instead he can simply talk to his granny, as he says, `*She being seventy must think about it, like every day*`.

Will and his Granny Tam have five short talks. At the end of each talk readers are invited to share their own thoughts and beliefs.

Using the book

The subjects discussed by Will and his Granny encourage further discussion. It does not matter if the young person reading the book asks questions to which there is no definitive answer, or to which the adult has no answer.

It is important to stress that death is a natural process for those who are very old and that ultimately dying happens to everyone. However often the most worrying aspect for young people is the knowledge that death can happen at any age. Talking about it openly can help children to articulate their concerns and lessen the fear of it.

At home

Parents, grandparents and carers can read this book at home with children. Older children may prefer to read it on their own. An adult may wish to read the book to help develop his or her own way of talking to a child about death and dying.

In the classroom

In a group, pupils can read the book all the way through or talk by talk. Then, under the guidance of a teacher they can share their thoughts, beliefs and concerns, as well as learn about those of their peers. Alternatively, discussion could be based on the children's written input which could be read out (anonymously, if preferred) to stimulate discussion.

Many people have strong religious beliefs about what happens after death. Some have none. It is important for children to realise there are many different beliefs and ideas. Discussion could be extended by learning how different cultures and faiths celebrate or mark death – for instance customs for funerals, burial and mourning etc.

It is essential to reassure young people at home or at school that thinking or talking about death and dying is neither unnatural nor strange. For the cycle of death is part of the cycle of life.

BOOKS

The following books are recommended for children of 8+

Death (The Journey of Life)
Sarah Levete
Rosen Central (2009)
ISBN 978-1435853515

Michael Rosen`s Sad Book
Michael Rosen & Quentin Blake
Walker Books (2008)
ISBN 978-0763641047

When People Die:Choices and Decisions
Pete Sanders and Steve Myers
Franklin Watts (2005)
ISBN 978-1596040762

When People Die: How can I deal with it?
Sally Hewitt
Franklin Watts (2007)
ISBN 978-0749670900

The following book is recommended for children of 12+

Bereavement (Real Life Issues)
Dee Pilgrims
Trotman and Co Ltd (2006)
ISBN 978-1844550999

ORGANISATIONS

Get Connected
UK Helpline for Young People
Support for emotional and physical well being
Helpline 0808 808 4994
Email: help@getconnected.org.uk   www.getconnected.org.uk

The Child Bereavement Charity
Aston House, High Street
West Wycombe HP14 3AG
01494 446648   www.childbereavement.org.uk

Winston's Wish
Charity for Bereaved Children
Westmoreland House, 80-86 Bath Road
Cheltenham   GL 53 7JT
General enquiries 01242 515 157
Helpline 08452 03 04 05
info@winstonswish.org.uk   www.winstonswish.org.uk

Cruse Bereavement Care
PO Box 800
Richmond TW9 1RG
020 8939 9530
Young People`s Helpline 0808 808 1677

www.rd4u.org.uk

National Children's Bureau
Childhood Bereavement Network
8 Wakley Street
London   EC1V 7QE
Helpline 020 7843 6309
Email: cbn@ncb.org.uk

www.childhoodbereavementnetwork.co.uk

THIRD AGE PRESS

. . . a unique publishing company

. . . an independent publishing company which recognizes that the period of life after full-time employment and family responsibility can be a time of fulfilment and continuing development . . . a time of regeneration

Third Age Press books are available by direct mail order from:

Third Age Press, 6 Parkside Gardens London SW19 5EY

Postage: please add 20% UK Sterling cheques payable to *Third Age Press*.

. . . or on order through book shops

Please send an SAE for full catalogue or visit our **website:**

www.thirdagepress.co.uk (website prices include postage)

Dianne Norton ~ Managing Editor   Email: dnort@globalnet.co.uk

A selection of our books that you may find of interest . . .

. . . is a series of booklets written by Dr Eric Midwinter that focus on the presentation of your unique life. These booklets seek to stimulate and guide your thoughts and words in what is acknowledged to be not only a process of value to future generations but also a personally beneficial exercise.

A Voyage of Rediscovery: a guide to writing your life story . . . is a 'sea chart' to guide your reminiscence & provide practical advice about the business of writing or recording your story.   36 pages   £4.50

Encore: a guide to planning a celebration of your life   An unusual and useful booklet that encourages you to think about the ways you would like to be remembered, hopefully in the distant future.   20 pages   £2.00

For details of all Third Age Press publications visit our website at www.thirdagepress.co.uk

Our Grandmothers, Our Mothers, Ourselves:
A CENTURY OF WOMEN'S LIVES

Eleven women who met through a U3A group exploring women's hidden social history talked, and then wrote, about their grandmothers, their mothers and their own lives. Their stories spanned the whole 20th Century, encompassed two world wars and many social and political changes affecting women. Through their discussions they crossed class and ethnic boundaries and exchanged their experiences of education, work and home life. They shared intimate family recollections honestly ~ uncovering affectionate as well as painful memories.

The book includes a section on the increasing use of life histories as a way of linking personal lives and public events, and a list of sources and further reading.   Charmian Cannon (Editor)   200 pages   £8.00

DEFINING WOMEN
. . . on mature reflection

Edited by Dianne Norton   150 pages   £12.50

The 'extraordinary ordinary women' invited to contribute to this anthology rose magnificently to the occasion, delving deep into their personal experiences and laying bare their innermost feelings as they met a variety of challenges. Gwen Parrish, U3A News

How to be a Merry Widow
~ life after death for the older lady

by Mary Rogers   158 pages   £12.50

• If you are looking for a politically correct, objective view of how to cope with bereavement - do **NOT** buy this book!

• This is a book about coming to terms with widowhood after the shock of bereavement has begun to ease.

• Mary Rogers writes with candour and humour, in a deeply personal style. She manages to be funny, moving and at the same time, practical.